The Titanium Mysteries Book 4:

Vampires

Ali Noel Vyain

Elsewhere

eISBN: 9780463058312

print ISBN: 9798201840006

1st edition printing

alinoelvyain.wordpress.com

Also By Ali Noel Vyain

The Colonies of Earth Series
The Colonies of Earth (Eris): Different
The Colonies of Earth (Venus): In Men's Shadows
The Colonies of Earth Series: Tales From Mars
The Colonies of Earth: The Colonies Will Be Independent
The Colonies of Earth: (Orcus): The Amazons Rise Up
The Colonies of Earth (Pluto): First Time
The Colonies of Earth (Saturn & Titan): Praying for Death
The Colonies of Earth (Mercury): This Strange, Wild Land
The Colonies of Earth (The Moon): The Crossroads
The Colonies of Earth (Triton): The Mistress
The Colonies of Earth (Neptune): The Plantation Owner
The Colonies of Earth (Ceres): The Vampire's Girlfriend
The Colonies of Earth (Titania): Vampire Struggles
The Colonies of Earth (Haumea): Aftermath
The Colonies of Earth: Box Set

The Starlover Series
Book 1: Project Earth
Book 2: Uncle & Niece
Book 3: Traveling Teenager
Book 4: Cassandra the Red Tiger
The Starlover Series Box Set

The Violet Series

The Guardian Series

The White Lion Unicorn Series

The Titanium Mysteries

Sir Socks Le Chat

Poetry

Non-Fiction Books

Contents

Chapter 1 The Attack

The police took pictures of the dead body. They took notes and samples. There was something odd about this body. The city of Tigerwood had never seen anything like it. The police had dealt with werewolf attacks, but clearly this was a different kind of murder. The officers shook their heads. Clearly it wasn't some sort of animal or were creature that had killed this person.

The obvious difference was the pale skin. Upon examination, they were able to find two tiny wounds in the neck. They sent the body to the morgue. A coroner would examine it soon. There was nothing else remarkable about the body. It appeared the person had lost too much blood.

But what had caused the two tiny wounds on the neck? The officers shook their heads. They finished up their notes. One made a phone call. The other said nothing.

"This is Detective Julian."

"Detective, we need you and Detective Zelda. We have just sent a body to the morgue. All we can tell you is that the skin is too pale and there are two tiny wounds on the neck. Do you have any idea what or who could have attacked them?"

"Hmm. I don't know. Doesn't sound like a were creature. That doesn't sound like the kind of wounds an animal could make. It must be someone humanoid."

The officer sighed. "We'll give you access to the coroner's report. We wish you still worked with us."

"Zelda, Zeta and I will look into it."

The officer disconnected. He sighed again. "I hope they can figure it out."

The other officer said, "If anyone can, they will. If this gets bad and beyond us, I wouldn't mind if the Guardians show up."

"Our superiors don't like them."

"They're fools. The Guardians share their knowledge. They aren't as shadowy as our superiors like to believe."

They left to go back to the station. The area had been cleared and they got what information they could from it. They waited for the coroner to send the report over. Neither spoke as they wrote up their initial findings. There wasn't much else to do at the moment.

Then they received the report. The most startling thing was the lack of blood left in the body. It was the cause of death. The wounds on the neck were puncture wounds. The blood had been sucked out of the body. The loss was so great so fast, that the person had died.

The officers finished reading the results and looked at each other. They knew what the monster was this time. It made their skin crawl.

"We have a vampire in Tigerwood."

"We need to tell the detectives."

"It's better that they call the Guardians. We don't need to lose our jobs."

They nodded to each other and sent off a copy of the report to Julian and Zelda. They waited and went on to other cases. There was nothing more they could do. They both hoped the private detectives could find the vampire and stop the killing spree.

Fear was something that was building up. Vampires were reputed to be hard to catch for humans and elves alike. But the Guardians were reputed to protect those who needed it the most. They were legend and they were real too. Sometimes it was hard to distinguish between the legend and the reality.

It wasn't long before it was all over the news. A new murderer was on the lose and people were scared. The police knew that it had to be a vampire this time. The weird thing was that the superiors weren't even denying the evidence this time. They didn't say much of anything about the dead body or the suspect.

There really wasn't much to say. Many knew it was a vampire. Many started to panic knowing there was a vampire hiding in the city where they wouldn't be able to know. Who was it? Where were they? When would they strike next?

Detectives Zelda and Julian read over the reports and watched the news. Neither said anything. They knew they could ask Zeta to research vampires and she would tell them everything she could find. They both agreed it had to be a vampire based on the evidence they had already.

It wasn't much yet, but it was something to start with. The detectives knew the police wouldn't be able to do much. They found it odd the superiors weren't denying the possibility of vampires this time. In fact they weren't saying much of anything.

Julian sent a message to Zeta requesting she study vampires and let them know what she found out. He and Zelda left to see where the police were earlier. They took their time walking to the crime scene. They showed their badges and the police let them look.

They studied the area without the body. They were able to confirm what the others before them had found out. They spent some time going over everything and seeing if they could see something the others didn't. Zelda bit her lip.

Julian asked her, "Well, what are you seeing this time?"

"I'm not sure there was a struggle here. Or if there was some play before the vampire bit their victim."

He looked down on the ground where she was looking. He nodded. "Yes, it isn't clear."

"I'm not sure it matters. The results are the same. But I do want to know how this vampire lured their victim and killed them."

He blinked. "Right. Sometimes the lines are blurry. In this case, we can't ask the victim now. I can't tell if they consented or not."

She looked up at him. "At least you get it. Let's go to the coroner's office."

He followed her. "Zeta says she's looking into the information on vampires. She'll tell us what she finds out tonight."

"Good."

It was a good little walk to the morgue. They were admitted to the coroner, who showed them the body.

Zelda said, "Just like the test says. They are pale. They lost that much blood from two puncture wounds in the neck?"

"Apparently, yes. I've never seen anything like it."

Julian blinked. "You've never dealt with vampires?"

"Not that I'm aware of. There are rumors some can be around us without feeding on us at all."

Zelda said, "Hmm. Interesting. Just like how not all were creatures are dangerous."

Julian nodded. "They know how to adapt and blend in with the rest of us."

They got what they came for and soon were leaving the building. Neither spoke for several minutes.

Zelda said, "I hope Zeta has better luck than what we're having right now."

"I'm sure she's studying and learning lots of new things. She did say she recently received a copy of the property legal documents."

"Oh, that should be interesting."

"Yeah, and she's supposed to be getting another opinion on her legs."

Chapter 2 Property Rights

Zeta blinked. She was sitting at her desk in her tiny house by herself. She concentrated on the legal document before her concerning the property she owned. It was clear from one of the clauses that her uncle Xavier couldn't take the property back. He had been involved in criminal activity which barred him from getting it now.

She frowned. He must have known this before he was so foolish and got himself into serious trouble. She read more and discovered another clause. One which stated she had to pass the property onto her children. If she didn't have children of her own, but had a sibling who did, those children could get the property from her too. Just as she had gotten it from her uncle. Seemed pretty easy to understand. She had no children of her own or any siblings. She could adopt, but she didn't think she could afford to. Or she could get pregnant. She wasn't so sure about that.

She wasn't even sure what Julian would think of that. They hadn't discussed having any children. She shrugged. She wasn't worried about it now. She was a bit shocked she even had a boyfriend who sometimes slept in her bed. Usually he slept in his tent outside.

She found his message. She answered him. Then she went back to the legal document. She gasped as she read something in another clause. Her parents and grandparents had been dead for years. She knew there was her uncle Xavier and her. But clearly in black and white this legal document mentioned another member of the family.

Uncle Xavier had a child of his own when he was much younger. Zeta blinked. She had no idea there was another relative. This one could inherit from her if he was still alive. She leaned back in her chair and thought. Did her parents know about this person? She thought back to when they were alive.

They had never mentioned she had a cousin. She blinked. This was really odd that there was another member of the family she wasn't told about. All she could figure was that this person would be quite a bit older than she was. It was possible that her uncle wasn't fully aware of this other person or was in some sort of denial. Hence Zeta was the one who held the property.

She blinked and looked back at the document. She would be doing more research today. She made notes on her cousin's name and possible age. He might not be so easy to find. She set aside that note and soon was looking up vampires.

She smiled when she found Herbert Mineur's notes. He was a valuable resource. He had documented evidence on were creatures, water nymphs and vampires. Other scientists were able to add more information to what he had discovered on Mars.

She kept reading. She nodded when she realized she had seen the body on the news and knew it had to had been killed by a vampire. She made notes. She would have plenty to tell her friends tonight around the fire.

The most important thing was that vampires couldn't live without blood. It was the only way for them to deal with their extreme anemia. But she found more than just what Herbert Mineur had noted. There were other scientists who pointed out that not all vampires hunted as clearly the one in Tigerwood was doing. Some were perfectly willing to buy donated blood or get special briefcases which produced blood for them.

She nodded and made more notes. So, not all vampires were evil or dangerous. Many knew about their condition and had learned to live among others without feeding on them. But clearly, when vampires hunted without regard for their prey, it could be bad. She sighed to see the notes on why the colony on Pluto had failed as it had.

A plague hadn't helped them. Two vampires had just made it worse. The first vampire was killed by his own girlfriend after he had raped a young woman. Then the remaining vampire had killed herself. So, the colonists were able to move on after that. They managed fairly well for nearly a whole generation until another vampire arrived and finished off the remaining colonists.

Zeta was upset. That was just rotten luck to have happen. They never had much of a chance even after they had created a vaccine for the disease. They had plenty of documented evidence that only people who went to visit needed to get the vaccine before they arrived or even just after they arrived so they would be okay.

She blinked. She needed food before they could study anything else. As she cooked her lunch, her mind wandered to her cousin she didn't know she had. According to what her uncle Xavier had told her, this person would still be alive. But where he was, was a question she couldn't answer yet. Soon she was eating and still thinking about her uncle Xavier being a father.

She couldn't see it. He certainly wasn't much of a father to her after her parents had died. She shook her head. It was useless for her to try and see her uncle like that. He was more absent than he was ever around. She had to finish growing up on her own. By herself. Her uncle didn't really pay attention. Zeta thought he must not have raised his own son.

Then who did? She finished eating and rinsed her dishes. She left them in the sink and sat back down at her desk. She made more notes to herself and found out more about vampires. She wrote up her notes she would be sharing with her friends later on.

She also scheduled an appointment to get her legs analyzed. It wasn't hard to set up the appointment. It was time to get another evaluation. They hadn't hurt as they used to. For years, she was walking better with the braces on and even around her tiny house without them a little bit. She smiled to herself. She had been told she would never be able to walk again and yet she did everyday.

She finished up her notes and smiled to herself. Perhaps there was some hope for her yet. Perhaps someday she wouldn't need the braces as much. Or perhaps not need them at all. She relaxed and thought good positive hopeful thoughts.

Zeta waited outside in the dark. She had just lit a fire. She was waiting for her best friends to show up. They were all in a detective agency together now. They were all partners. She stared into the fire and watched the flames. Her mind wandered. She wasn't aware of her friends when they sat down in their accustomed chairs.

"Hey, Zeta." Julian smiled at her.

She didn't respond. Zelda raised an eyebrow. Julian wave one of his hands in front of Zeta's face. She jumped back and blinked.

"Oh, there you are," said Zeta.

Zelda smiled. "I hope you weren't waiting long for us."

Zeta shook her head no. "I did find out about vampires as you requested. The main problem is that they have severe anemia, which requires blood for their diet."

Julian cringed.

"It also makes their skin paler than it is for the rest of us. They also tend to speed up."

Zelda said, "Great. So, someone who needs blood to survive and can move faster than the rest of us."

Zeta nodded. "Actually, they aren't faster than all of us."

Julian said, "What?"

Zeta smiled. "Vampires tend to be faster, but some people have a brain illness known as Attention Deficient Hyperactive Disorder. They can move just as fast as vampires."

Zelda said, "Sounds like the Princess Claire Rose Lutin could have that."

Zeta nodded. "Yes, and she had anemia before she was born. Hence her pale skin."

Julian said, "I see. Isn't she immune to the virus?"

Zeta nodded. "She is. It runs in her family. Although she herself is still prone to anemia and paleness. If she is exposed to the vampire virus, it can still affect her skin coloring and lower her iron count. It probably has a strong effect on her ADHD too."

Zelda chuckled. "Wow. No wonder she was chosen to fight against her great grandfather."

Julian said, "So, we're looking for a vampire and we might need help from the Guardians."

Zeta blinked. "Some Guardians are vampires. They could help us with this dangerous one."

Zelda asked, "How do the non-dangerous vampires feed?"

"They get or buy donated blood. Or they get special briefcases which produce the blood they need."

Julian said, "So, they don't need to hunt. Or even ask permission. We have donated blood on hand most of the time. That's at least some comfort."

Zeta asked, "How many victims so far?"

Zelda answered, "Just one that we know of."

Zeta said, "If this person is having blood lust, there will be a lot more victims."

Zelda sighed. "We couldn't tell if there was a struggle. We can't tell if the vampire raped their victim or if the victim consented."

Zeta sighed. "I suppose that would be hard to determine. It would depend upon the vampire. Some do have sex with their victims. Some do commit rape too. There are some documented cases of both."

Julian cringed. "That's not good."

Zeta shook her head. "Sometimes even when the victim consents, they aren't fully aware of what the vampire is doing until their blood is gone."

Zelda said, "And they die from too much blood loss."

No one spoke for several minutes.

Julian looked at Zeta. "Did you find anything about your legs?"

"I have an appointment next week. I am a bit nervous. I remember I was told I would never be able to walk again."

Julian smiled. "You do walk a lot."

"Not without crutches or my braces."

Zelda said, "Well, sometimes a second opinion does help out. I hope you can get rid of the braces and the crutches."

"I hope so too."

Julian said, "What's the matter? Did you learn something else today?"

"Yes, apparently I have a cousin no one told me about."

Zelda sat up. "What? Who is this cousin?"

"A son of my uncle Xavier."

Julian raised an eyebrow. "So, Xavier had other secrets."

"I doubt he raised his own son."

Zelda asked, "Do you have any information on your cousin?"

"Just a name. He has to be older than I am. That's all I know so far."

Julian pulled out his tablet computer. "Okay, what's the name?"

"Peter Xavier Tobus."

Julian put the name into a database. "Oh, he is the son of your uncle and a woman named Cynthia Tobus. She raised him by herself."

Zelda raised an eyebrow. "Does he know his father?"

Julian answered, "I don't know. Doesn't say. Just said he was raised by her. So, it has to do with the property doesn't it?"

Zeta nodded. "Yes, I can only pass it on to any children I may have or a sibling of mine may have. I don't have any siblings and if I don't have any children of my own then it could go to my cousin. I can't sell it."

Zelda asked, "What is there is no heir?"

"I don't know. I couldn't understand that last clause. It was a bit confusing. It just might be me. But I do know my uncle can't have the property because he has been convicted of criminal activity."

Julian said, "I see. Well, there's no criminal record for your cousin. Could his mother inherit in a weird scenario?"

"I don't know. Possibly. You two might be able to get if from me. But there would be certain restrictions. That's the part I couldn't understand. I can't just sell it or give it away."

Zelda nodded. "Zeta, don't worry about the property right now. And please don't feel the need to have any children any time soon."

Zeta smiled. "I'm not sure I want any."

Zelda smiled. "I'm not sure Julian is ready to have any either."

Julian chuckled. "Okay, I get it. I haven't decided either. But if it happens, I'm not backing out of the relationship or the responsibility."

Both Zelda and Zeta smiled at him.

Chapter 3 Another Attack

The police officer sighed. He wasted no time contacting detectives Zelda and Julian to the scene. The body had the same marks on it as the other one did. It was just as pale too. It was several minutes later before the detectives arrived.

Zelda asked, "Any signs of a struggle as last time?"

"Oh, yeah. I think there was something." He pointed to the marks on the ground.

She nodded and looked to Julian.

Julian said, "Yeah, we couldn't determine if it was rape or consensual. It could be either way."

Zelda turned back to the officers. "There are documented cases of vampires raping their prey and having sex with others."

"Eh, okay. So, you agree it's definitely a vampire."

The detectives nodded.

"Great. I'm surprised our superiors aren't saying anything about this. Are you going to call the Guardians?"

Julian answered, "That would probably be a good idea. Unless someone on the force has ADHD."

The officer blinked. "Why would that matter?"

Julian answered, "They would have a fighting chance to be as fast as the vampire."

"Oh! I never knew that."

Zelda said, "I don't think most people would know that."

"Right. Well, we won't tell on you if call on the Guardians. We can use all the help we can get."

Julian said, "You just don't want to lose your jobs."

"Yes, that's it."

Julian smiled. "Well, fortunately, for you, we have connections and we're independent. We won't lose our jobs if we contact them."

The body was taken away to the morgue. They made more notes and waited for the coroner's report. Julian and Zelda walked away from the crime scene.

Zelda said, "I think Zeta is going to her appointment about now."

Julian nodded. "I hope it's good news."

"And if it's not?"

He shrugged. "We'll deal with it."

She smiled.

Zeta checked into her appointment and waited in the waiting room. She had just heard there was another victim. She hoped her friends were finding more clues. She told them all she had found out in one session. There could be more information, but she couldn't be sure after the major sources she had found.

Soon it was her turn. A nurse led her to the machine. Zeta laid down on the table. The nurse removed her braces. Then they moved the table into the machine where it scanned her legs. The nurse read the screen.

The nurse blinked. "I saw the records. The original doctor thought you wouldn't be able to walk and yet you do with crutches or braces. This is amazing. I know you can't see it in that position, but your legs have healed up well. I think someone made a mistake about you and your legs."

"What?" asked Zeta.

"Your legs are in much better shape than the doctor thought they would be. Do you do any regular exercising?"

"Yes. I tend to go for walks with the braces on."

"Well, your muscles have recovered well. You might be able to walk without the braces before long."

"What? How is that possible?"

"Sometimes the body heals slowly. There was a lot of damage to your legs in the accident. That is quite clear from the records. You also didn't give up on yourself. You built up your arm muscles to help you learn how to walk again."

"Will I be able to run again?"

The nurse moved the table out of the machine. "Yes. You could dance if you wanted to."

Zeta smiled. "I don't know about dancing. But running might be a good thing to be able to do."

The nurse put her braces back on her legs. "But take it slow. The braces have helped you walk as much as you can now. I wouldn't recommend letting go of them just yet. Do you have railing in your house?"

"Yes."

"Try practicing walking around your house without the braces. But use the railing if you need it."

"Okay."

Zeta walked back to her house to find Julian cooking dinner for the two of them.

"Hi, Jule."

"Hi, Zeta. How did go? You're smiling. It must be good news."

She nodded. "I was told my legs have healed up well enough that I could try walking around my house without the braces. But I should use the railing if I need it. They think I might be able to run eventually or even dance if I wanted to."

Julian smiled at her. "Running would be useful in our line of work. Although being able to dance would be nice too."

"What? You mean dancing with you."

"Yes, dancing close."

She tickled him and he laughed. "I never was that coordinated. I can't promise that."

"Okay." He put his arms around her.

She put her arms around him. He got both of them to sway a bit.

In her own tiny house, Zelda smiled to see her friends close together. She had just sent a message to the Guardians about the latest murderer loose in Tigerwood. She was waiting for a response and wasn't sure how long it would be. It was just the same site as they had used before where people can request help.

Zelda sighed. She wondered if the Guardians had to sift through lots of weird requests that aren't worth their time. She shook her head. She glanced at her friends again. She wondered if there was someone out there for her. Or was she better off on her own?

Her tablet beeped. She checked it. A Guardian had just answered her. She blinked. She couldn't believe her luck. Both Sam Oranglov and Felicia had answered. Zelda knew they were both vampires now. Soon she had both on her screen staring at her with seemingly cold eyes.

"Detective Zelda, we just saw the reports you sent us. We agree it is a vampire in your city. We can be there by tomorrow."

Zelda nodded. "That will help out. Zeta says perhaps if anyone has ADHD, they might be able to go after the vampire."

Sam nodded. "That's possible. But I wouldn't recommend it. They would be risking their lives."

Zelda raised an eyebrow. Aren't you risking your lives by going after a vampire?"

"Yes, but we are vampires, so we have a better chance of catching them and taking care of them."

Zelda smiled. "That is true. I'm just surprised that you two answered my message."

Felicia smiled. "We don't always have assignments. Other Guardians tend to be afraid of us. So, we tend to monitor vampire activity and make sure of those who are safe and those who aren't. We even help those who don't want to harm others."

Zelda nodded. "Just like the werewolf we dealt with who helped the young man cope with his condition."

Felicia nodded. "Many don't choose to become vampires and don't know how to cope. We try to catch them early so they can live without hunting and harming others. Were creatures aren't quite the same as they may not know until they are fully grown as was the case with the one you met."

"Do you need anything else from us?"

Sam answered, "No, not unless new evidence appears."

"Okay. We'll be in contact."

Chapter 4 A Cousin

Zeta was out walking by herself. She looked around as her mind digested what she had been studying. One thing which shocked her was that there had been a child before her. Someone she never knew or even heard of. She sighed to realize her uncle Xavier had a child that perhaps her parents didn't know about. She knew he hadn't raise the child either.

She had on her braces as she walked. Later she would take them off and try walking around her tiny house. For now she wanted to clear her head. She had tried to get in contact with her cousin. He hadn't answered her back. She wasn't sure she had the correct contact information for him. She wasn't even sure if his mother was still alive.

Zeta shook her head. It was possible his mother was still alive, but she seemed to be elusive for some reason. Zeta knew some people didn't like to be tracked and refused to have social media accounts. She blinked. Her cousin's mother was probably one of those people. Zeta wondered if Xavier was in contact with either of them.

Knowing her uncle as well as she did, he probably wasn't regular with his messaging or calling. She sighed remembered what she had found out about his full activities. She wasn't surprised he was now in prison paying for the crimes he had committed over the years.

Soon Zeta was feeling better. She realized she was nervous because of the property restrictions. Whoever had set them up knew what they were doing. There was no way she could sell the property if she had wanted to. Without any children of her own, it would be next to impossible to pass it on to someone else.

She had to meet her cousin. There was no way she could make any decisions as to what would happen to the property if she were to die unless she knew her cousin. She wondered if her cousin knew about the property or even her uncle.

She sighed and walked back home. She blinked. There were other people out walking. Some seemed happy. Others seemed upset. It was just another day. Zeta looked forward to more reading as her friends were studying clues and track down a vampire.

She got inside the gate and walked to her house as the gate shut itself behind her. She could hear her friends discussing the latest case as she passed Zelda's house. She smiled to herself. Both seemed to be happy when they were working on a case.

Zeta got inside her house and sat down at her desk. She found a message from her cousin waiting for her. She checked it. It simply said he was willing to meet her in a local cafe. He wanted to hear some stories about his dad. She blinked and reread the message. She answered him stating she would be happy to meet him at the cafe. They arranged for a day and time.

She sat back and blinked. She bit her lip lightly. She wasn't sure what to expect from this person. Would he resemble her uncle Xavier in any way? She frowned. She would soon find out. She picked up her tablet and read her book. Soon she was lost inside the world the writer had created.

In the other tiny house, Zelda blinked. "Zeta is home."

Julian stopped and looked out the window. "Good. I wonder what's happened now."

"She looks busy."

"I know. So, you said you were able to get a hold of two Guardians this time."

"Yes, and you might be shocked who answered this time."

"Who?"

"Sam Oranglov and Felicia."

He blinked. "Two Guardians who became vampires!"

She nodded.

"Wow. I think our chances of survival have just increased." She smiled.

"Okay, so when will they get here?"

"Soon."

"Oh, right, Felicia is one of the best pilots around."

She chuckled. "Has Zeta asked what you think about having children?"

"No. Why would she?"

"Just checking. I think the restrictions on the property are on her mind."

"Oh…"

"Well, what do you think?"

"I don't know. Perhaps I'm still too young."

She laughed. "People younger than us have children every-day."

"Yes, I know."

"Or are you just too focused on your work?"

"That's part of it."

"And what else?"

"I'm not the one who gets pregnant. I'd have to ask someone else to carry the child for me. I don't know if I have to right to ask."

She sat down. "Very good. I knew I didn't have to worry about you with any woman. All I had to worry about is if she wouldn't be good for you. I know Zeta well enough to know you'll be fine."

He shook his head as he smiled. "You're like the sister I never had."

She laughed. "You don't have any sisters?"

"Nope. I'm an only child."

"Must be nice."

He shrugged. "I only know what my friends told me about having sisters. Some liked their sisters. Others weren't too sure of them."

"Sounds about right."

"And what about you? Ever wanted to have any children of your own?"

"No, not really. I'd be happy to be an aunt."

"Well, if Zeta and I have any, you can be aunt to them."

She smiled.

"Oh, wait, do you miss having a girlfriend?"

She sighed.

"Oh, I'm sure there's someone out there for you."

"You're such a hopeless romantic."

"I'm just hopeless when it comes to Zeta."

"Good. I am happy for the two of you. I do wish I had someone, but we have important work to do too. Sometimes that doesn't work out well with a romantic relationship."

"Unless, she works with us too?"

She shook her head. She chuckled. "Go see Zeta. It will be some time before the Guardians get here."

"Okay, if I run into any women who find you attractive, I'll introduce you."

She shook her head. He heard her laugh as he left her house to see Zeta. He let himself in. He didn't try to be quiet about it. She turned her head to see him. She smiled. He walked over to her and leaned down to kiss her forehead.

He sat down next to her. "So, what's going on?"

"Oh, I'm meeting my cousin in a few days. I don't know what

to expect."

"Are you afraid he'll remind you of Xavier?"

She nodded.

"Well, he might have some of Xavier's physical features. There's not telling if he acts anything at all like your uncle."

"I know that, but I never heard of him. He might resent that I have the property instead of him."

He nodded. "Zelda thought it was the property restrictions that was upsetting you. She went on to tease me again about having children."

She smiled. "I'm not in any rush."

"I told her I hadn't thought much about it. I don't know if I have any right to ask."

"Good point. That would be tricky for you since you can't get pregnant."

He smiled at her. "Zelda and I can shadow you if you're really nervous."

"We're meeting at the cafe over near the fire station."

"Oh, okay. Do you think you could get out easily if there's any trouble?"

"Yes. I still haven't tried to run, but I should be able to get out and away."

"Okay. You won't be mad if we show up too?"

She shook her head.

"Good. We'll stay back. We'll be there if you need any backup."

"Okay. That's fine. I could use the moral support meeting him."

"Oh, and we have two vampire Guardians coming here."

"What? When?"

"Very soon. At least they are on our side. I told Zelda our chances of survival have just increased."

"Of course they have. Who are they?"

"Sam Oranglov and Felicia."

"Oh! He used to be human and she was a fairy. They grew up together and became a couple later in life after she had reached adolescence."

"Is there an age difference between them?"

She shook her head. "No, they were best friends as children. I know you want to ask. He went through adolescence about two decades before she did."

"So, he robbed the fairy cradle."

She laughed. "I suppose he did in a way. They are about the same age."

He laughed with her. "I'm glad we don't have that problem."

She climbed on to his lap.

He put his arms around her waist. "To what do I owe this pleasure to?"

"You're just lucky right now." She leaned in and kissed him.

He kissed her back.

Chapter 5 Vampire?

Zeta sighed. It was nearly time for the meeting with her cousin. She wasn't sure what to expect. At least they were meeting in a local cafe. If anything were to go wrong, she would be able to get out easily. Just the same she was comforted by the near presence of her two best friends. She got herself a tea and found a table. Julian and Zelda got themselves some drinks and found a table near her.

None of them had to wait very long. Soon a male elf approached Zeta. He had a hat on. He greeted her and sat down.

"Zeta, is it?"

"Yes."

"I'm Peter Xavier Tobus. Pleased to meet a cousin of mine."

"Hi. I understand my uncle Xavier is your father."

"Yes, he is. Did you ever see him much when you were growing up?"

She shook her head.

"Hmm. I didn't either. My mom told me about him." He took a sip of his drink. "She told me about their relationship. I did see him from time to time, but it seemed rare when he did show up."

"It was like that with me too."

"I did hear you and your parents were in a bad accident which killed them and left you crippled. Although you don't seem that way to me."

"My legs have healed up well over the years."

"Oh? That's good. Can you dance?"

She laughed. "No. I can walk though."

"I see."

Zelda made some notes on her tablet. She sent a message to Julian. He read it and blinked. He looked at her and over at Peter. Julian looked back at Zelda and sent her a message back. She read it and nodded. They both kept an eye on Peter and Zeta.

"I know my dad is in prison for some things he's done. I wasn't aware he was up to trouble like that."

"I didn't know either although I always wondered what he did for money. Whenever I had asked him, he evaded the question."

"That sounds like him. There were plenty of questions I asked him and he wouldn't tell me anything."

She sighed. She wondered what her cousin would want her to answer.

"He never told me about you."

"No? I guess I shouldn't be surprised by that."

"I found out later. That's how I know about your parents and you. I know you're working with two famous detectives too. You're a writer."

"Yes, that's correct."

"Do you like working with them?"

"Yes. I mainly write up the cases after they solve them. I also do research when they need to know things for the cases they're working on."

"You sound happy with your work."

"I am. I don't want to do anything else."

He smiled at her. She couldn't see his eyes, but she could see his pale hands. They were paler than hers. She thought he had some of her uncle's mannerisms.

He continued, "I suppose you have questions for me."

She nodded. "Is your mom still alive?"

"Yes."

"How is she doing?"

"Fine. She's happy. She doesn't go out much these days. She likes her privacy."

"Hence why she doesn't have any social media profiles."

"Exactly." He paused to finish his drink. "Would you like to meet her?"

The hair on the back of her neck stood up. Both Zelda and Julian watched closely.

"Oh, I don't know yet. I am pretty busy."

"No rush. She's not going anywhere anytime soon. She tends to stay at home."

She blinked. She felt she needed to see his eyes. There was something she was missing. She finished her tea. "Well, it's been good to meet you. We'll have to get together again soon."

"Likewise. It's good to know a writer who has her head screwed on straight."

"Uh, thanks."

"You're welcome. I'll be in touch." He stood up and left the table.

She watched him go. When she could no longer see him, she let out a sigh. Julian and Zelda stood up and sat down at her table.

"Zeta, you okay?" asked Julian.

"I don't know. I think I missed something important about him."

Zelda said, "He didn't take off his hat."

Zeta nodded. "I couldn't see his eyes. I needed to see them. His hands are paler than mine."

Zelda nodded. "We both noticed that. We heard what you both said too."

Julian said, "I wondered why he asked if you wanted to meet his mom. You just met him. It seems a bit soon."

Zeta sighed. "My cousin and I aren't dating."

Zelda said, "No, of course not. It did sound odd to my ears too. We both saw you react to it in a bad way. You knew instinctively that wasn't a good question to ask."

Julian sighed. "Could he know about the property?"

Zelda blinked. "If he knows you have it and he could get it from you? That's a possibility. It's hard to say right now. We don't have enough information."

Zeta said, "But uncle Xavier did mention there was someone else who could own the property."

Julian said, "Right, he did. So, it's possible your cousin knows about the property and perhaps the legal restrictions on it."

Zeta sighed. "I hope my cousin isn't a vampire."

Both Zelda and Julian gasped and stared at her.

Julian said, "That's what you were missing."

Zeta nodded. "He wouldn't take off his hat. Perhaps he can't take the sun as well as we can. He is awfully pale even if he is a cousin."

Zelda stood up. "Perhaps we better go home for now. I'm sure you need to exercise your legs, Zeta."

Zeta blinked. She and Julian stood up. The trio walked home together. Zeta was pensive. Zelda and Julian were wary of any-one near them.

Peter smiled as he entered the apartment. His mother Cynthia was sitting on the sofa.

"I take it the meeting went well."

"Yes, mom, it did. She seems to be all that we thought she would be."

She smiled at him. The curtains were drawn throughout the apartment. She was just as pale as he was. "With Xavier out of the way, there's just her."

"The property is currently solely hers."

"But you could do something about that. I'm sure you could convince her to let you have the property."

"She and her friends are living on it, remember?"

"Yes, I remember. But we can get rid of them."

"How? They are famous and contribute highly to the city. They would be missed if something happened to them."

"We'll think of something."

"I hope so. In the meantime, perhaps I will see my cousin again. She is pretty."

She laughed.

"You find that amusing?"

"Why not? The rules are different for us than they are for others not like us."

He smiled. "I know. That's why I told you I think she's pretty. I wonder what she would be like in bed." He sat down next to his mother. "But that will have to wait for now. I take it my dad doesn't know what we've become?"

She shook her head. "I didn't tell him anything. Besides, he's in prison. I doubt I could go visit him right now."

"There is an old fashioned way of writing on paper and sending letters."

"Psha! Why bother? I don't care for paper anymore. He was stupid enough to get himself caught."

His smile grew. "I don't feel inclined to tell him anything

either. He neglected me while I was growing up."

"At least you love the one who raised you." She stroked his cheek.

"Of course I do, but I need more than just you."

"Oh, do you now? Just a plaything or two or something more serious?"

"I haven't decided. I've been sampling a few lately, but I haven't found what I'm looking for."

"What about your cousin?"

"Ah, that's the questions isn't it? It would be great if we could get together. Then there would be no questions about the property."

"Now there's the beginning of a good idea."

"Alright, I'll think about it and make her an offer."

"That's my boy."

Chapter 6 More Attacks

Felicia landed their ship in the spaceport just outside of Tigerwood. She and Sam lived on the ship. They didn't need to get a hotel room or rent an apartment for now. It was dark when they had landed. Sam contacted Detective Zelda. Her face soon appeared on the screen in front of them.

"I hope you have good news."

Sam smiled. "We do. We've just arrived at the spaceport. We've also have been reviewing the data you sent us. We'd like to meet up with you and your partners soon."

"That can be arranged. You're welcome to come here. We tend to sit around a fire pit at night."

"That will work for us. Just send us the address."

"Okay. You can come now. I know my partners do want to see you."

Zelda and Julian stood around making notes on the new victims. They read the coroner's reports on all of them. They even got input from the police as well. They made their notes and were sharing what they knew. It was getting bad. Now there were five dead bodies. They wondered if there would be more and when they would happen.

They left the latest crime scene to walk home. Zelda sent a message to Zeta about the Guardians who were on their way. Neither spoke as they walked back to their home. It seemed like a long walk, but when they reached the gate, they could see Zeta walking through her tiny house.

Zelda asked, "Does she have her braces on?"

"I don't think so. She has her arms up for balance. I think she's practicing walking without them."

Zelda smiled. "I'll get the fire pit ready. I don't know when our guests will be arriving."

"I'll check on Zeta." Julian went inside Zeta's house. He smiled at her.

She turned around. She still had her arms up. "I guess my balance isn't too bad, but it's slow doing this."

"You're not used to trying to walk without your braces."

She nodded. "Yes, that's it. I've gotten so used to the braces that I wasn't sure I'd ever be able to do without them."

He blinked. "How do your legs feel?"

"Fine."

"Can you bend your knees more?"

"Well, I suppose I could try." She couched. "Oh, that feels weird without the braces."

"Just be careful. Your legs may not be used to that kind of movement."

She reached out for a railing. "Yeah, I do need to be careful. But I can walk a little bit without the braces." She held onto the railing as she did some stretches testing her legs without the braces. "Ah, this will take some time to get full movement back."

He smiled at her. There was a beep alerting them to visitors at the gate. He checked it.

"Our guests are here." He let them in. "Are you ready?"

"Let me put the braces back on for now."

"Okay."

She walked back to her bed and slipped the braces on and then stood back up. "Okay, that feels more normal. I don't want to overdo it with my legs."

"Good idea."

They stepped out of the tiny house and sat down in their usual seats around the fire pit. Their visitors had just sat down. Zelda was sharing more information with them about the latest victims. They studied the new data and made their own notes.

Felicia said, "There's no telling how many vampires there could be."

Sam asked, "Do you think there could be more than one?"

"Yes."

The elves cringed.

Zelda said, "Zeta, I haven't mentioned your cousin just yet."

"Oh, I just met him the other day. He wore a hat and wouldn't take it off. His hands were paler than mine are."

Sam asked, "Do you think he could be a vampire?"

Zeta answered, "Possibly. I don't know for sure."

Felicia said, "So, there was no physical contact between the two of you?"

Zeta shook her head. "But he asked me if I wanted to meet his mother. I never even knew he existed until my uncle mentioned there was someone else in the family. My cousin was raised by his mother and not his father. My cousin said he does know his father, but never saw him much growing up."

Felicia said, "I see. Would your uncle know if his own son is a vampire?"

Zeta blinked. "Probably not. My cousin knows my uncle is in prison now."

Sam said, "The bodies are starting to pile up. I'd say it sounds like a blood lust has started."

Felicia said, "I'd agree. The people in this city are in danger including the three right here."

Sam smiled at Felicia. "Then we'll have to come up with a plan to trap the vampire or vampires as soon as possible."

Julian said, "It appears all the victims liked to go to the downtown area where the nightclubs are. Many people are saying they've seen the victims dancing at some of the clubs."

Zelda said, "Or at least that's what many are saying. Claiming they've seen the victims in the area many times before they died."

Felicia said, "That would be a good place to look for the vampire. But it is dangerous to go after dark. Vampires are very strong in the dark."

Zeta said, "But we have to catch them. If this is a lead, then we should follow it."

Sam said, "Then we'll follow you three. It should be easy for us to blend in. We are a couple and people won't question us hanging out together."

Zelda said, "Okay, then we'll do it tomorrow night. I can question people as a single woman hanging out with her best friends who are a couple too."

Julian smiled, "Perhaps you can find a date, Zel."

Zelda shook her head as she smiled. "We have a case to solve."

Felicia raised an eyebrow and then smiled.

Sam smiled too. "Zeta, is this normal between them?"

Zeta smiled. "Yes. They tend to act like brother and sister. I know they're not related, but they have worked together for years."

Sam said, "Good that will help solve this case."

Felicia said, "The Guardian who worked with you already said you were a great team of detectives. So, you have a good reputation with us."

Zelda smiled. "Good. We may need your help again depending upon what we find."

Sam said, "We may contact you if we need information or if we are looking for someone you may be looking for too."

Julian said, "We'll work with you. We've got nothing to hide."

Chapter 7 The Offer

Zelda, Julian, and Zeta went out for a walk to a local venue. They decided it was best to go at night because it was the scene of where the vampire had found their prey. Julian and Zeta held hands. Zelda walked near them wondering if she would meet someone tonight. It was a possibility.

Sam and Felicia held hands as they trailed behind the elves. They watched everyone carefully. They could see things others tended to miss. Those little tell-tale signs of another vampire. The stars speckled the sky. They sniffed the air and watched everyone around them.

Zelda shook her head. "Jul and Zeta, you are quite silly now." She chuckled. "You're getting out of hand."

Zeta laughed.

Julian smiled. "Zel, see anyone you'd like to get to know better?"

Zelda smiled. She said nothing as they made their way through the crowd. They hadn't seen a sign of any vampires other than the two following them.

"Zeta!"

Zeta, Julian and Zelda stopped.

Zeta blinked. "Hi, Peter."

Peter smiled. He wasn't wearing a hat now. He was still rather pale. "I'm so glad to see you. Are these your friends?"

Zeta nodded.

"Hello, Zeta's friends. I'm her cousin Peter." He turned back to Zeta. "I have an offer to make you. Come with me." He motioned for her to follow.

Julian squeezed Zeta's hand. He and Zelda nodded to her as soon as Peter walked away. They soon followed him. He led them inside one of the nightclubs and into a private room. He sat down and waited for them to sit down.

Sam and Felicia saw where they went. They didn't enter the private room. Instead they stopped nearby where they could hear and danced close together. Their hearing picked up on what was said inside the private room.

"Zeta, I know about the property and I would like to make you an offer."

Julian and Zelda gasped.

Zeta blinked. "My friends and I live on the property."

"Oh? Well, of course you do. I was hoping we could own it together. My mother and I could then live on the property as well."

The hairs on the back of Zeta's neck stood up. "I suppose there might be room for you if you were willing to live in small house."

"Small?"

"There are two tiny houses on the property already. It's not that big as I'm sure you already know."

"Why not have everyone living in a mansion?"

Zeta sighed. "That doesn't sound very comfortable. I think we like to have our own space."

"You could have that in a mansion."

Zeta shook her head. "It wouldn't be the same. We do like to sit around a fire pit at night. But we still want our own space too. I think it's normal and healthy to have some privacy."

Peter sighed. "But we could have a mansion together. We could be a real family."

"Family? I barely know you and my uncle is in prison."

"We could rule this city together. Perhaps you'd like to be in charge?"

Zeta shook her head no. Zelda and Julian watched him carefully. Something seemed wrong.

Julian asked, "What about Zelda and me? Would we be allowed to live in the mansion too?"

Peter looked at the elf. "That depends on your attitude."

Zeta said, "What? You would dare to kick my friends out onto the street?"

"Zeta, dear, they aren't like us. They aren't family."

Zeta blinked. "What is family? Uncle Xavier wasn't that great and wasn't around. My parents died when I was still a minor. I don't know you or your mother."

Peter sighed. "My mother and I could give you eternal life and power that puts us above the law. Your friends may not respect that or get what it means. If they don't submit to us, they can't live in the mansion."

Zeta frowned. "I don't want a mansion on my property. I don't want to share it with you or your mother. I will not throw my friends out on the street."

"Zeta, be reasonable."

Sam and Felicia slipped inside the room silently.

Felicia said, "Peter, how long have you been a vampire?"

Peter gasped. "How did you know?"

Felicia smiled revealing her fangs. "It's so easy to identify a vampire after you've become one." She raised her wings. "And I can do what you can't."

Peter's eyes widened. "You have wings? How is that possible?"

"I was a fairy once."

"A fairy? Fairies can become vampires?"

Felicia nodded. She lowered her wings. She stepped closer to Peter. She walked around him. He held still. She took out her scanner and ran it behind him. She made some mental notes and put the scanner away. "Where do you get your blood? No vampire can survive without blood."

Peter scowled. "None of your business."

Felicia walked around to face him. "Correction, it is everyone's business where vampires get their blood. Especially when people are found dead with vampire bite marks on their necks. If that is you killing people, we Guardians have an answer for you." She stared him down.

Peter slammed a fist into the table. "I don't have to listen to this."

Sam raised an eyebrow. "Actually, you do. She and I are vampires and we don't feed on people. We get donated or synthetic blood. We don't hunt. It's against the Guardian code to hunt for blood."

Zeta said, "I wonder if his mother is a vampire..." Her eyes were big and wild.

Peter jumped up. He grabbed Zeta and ran off with her. Julian and Zelda screamed. Sam ran after them. Felicia flew out of the club. Julian and Zelda ran out of the club. They didn't stop running. They just followed the vampire fairy as best as they could.

The vampires were faster than the detectives, but they could see Felicia flying above them. They followed her all the way to an apartment tower. They entered the building and didn't know where to go next. Zeta was no where to be seen. Nor were Peter or Sam.

Felicia landed in front of the detectives and smiled at them. "Come with me. I know where they are." She grabbed them and flew up building. She laughed as she flew up the tower. Julian and Zelda screamed. This was not what they had in mind for a night on the town.

Felicia landed the three of them on a balcony. She let go of the detectives and let them breathe as she checked the sliding door. It was locked. She slammed her fist into the glass, which scattered on impact. Zelda and Julian just stared. The glass fell to the floor and revealed Peter and Sam fighting over Zeta who was held captive by Cynthia, Peter's mother.

Cynthia smiled at the newcomers standing on the balcony. "Welcome. You're just in time. I see you brought us more prey for tonight. That does help out. There's one for each of us. Unless they decide to join us and live forever." She laughed.

Chapter 8 The Police Response

The officers reviewed the data from the current open case. They were afraid there would be more bodies before long. They tried to do a DNA match on a possible murderer. They knew they were looking for a vampire. They were well aware that many vampires tended to hide and didn't get their DNA done for any reason. Vampires don't get medical exams unless forced to.

They frowned. They couldn't find any matches. Their superiors came over to ask them about the case.

"So, is the murderer really a vampire?"

"We're afraid so."

"I see. So what do we tell the people?"

"The truth I would guess."

"But this could cause a huge panic."

"Any serial killer can cause a huge panic. I don't think it matters whether it's a human or an elf or a vampire."

The superior sighed. "You have a point. If we look at history, serial killers in general tend to create panic. Okay, what do you have so far?"

"We know it's a vampire killing these people by sucking their blood out of them too fast. We also know the victims tend to hang out in the same nightclubs."

"So, the vampire finds their victims at the nightclubs?"

"Yes, at night because vampires can't stand sunlight very well."

"Right. How are we going to catch them?"

The officers shrugged their shoulders.

"I see. So, could I warn people to stay away from the vampire if they can?"

"That seems to be the best option we have."

"Okay. I'll do that. I'm holding a press conference in a few minutes." The superior paused. "One more thing. Did either of you contact the Guardians about this case?"

The officers shook their heads no.

"Good. We don't need to look weak in front of the people." The superior left to get ready for the press conference.

The officers blinked and looked at each other.

"Good thing we told the detectives."

"I'm sure they've contacted the Guardians by now."

"And we still have our jobs."

"For now. If we get fired, we can offer our services to the Xenocryst Agency."

"That's a good back up plan just in case."

They blinked. Reports were flocking to the newsroom at the police station. The officers got up to go and watch in the back. The anticipation was overwhelming. Many officers stood around in the back of the room as reports filed into the seats in front of the podium.

The chief of police approached the podium. They blinked and addressed the crowd. "As you know, we have several victims from a new serial killer. From the evidence, I can tell you it's a vampire who is draining their victims dry. We the police recommend that you be careful at night especially around the nightclubs. This particular vampire stalks their victims in that area."

Everyone was stunned by the announcement. Several officers mumbled in the back of the room. Reporters took notes.

"Okay, we are open to questions as I'm sure you all have them."

A reporter asked, "Have you contacted the Guardians for help?"

The superior blinked. "No. The Guardians are a myth. We are on our own for this case. We suggest that you avoid anyone who is very pale and only goes out after dark. As I'm sure many of you know vampires can't handle sunlight as the rest of us can."

Another report asked, "Will you try and catch the vampire?"

"I don't know that we have anyone on the force who can catch a vampire."

One of the officers spoke up, "Well, if we have anyone on the force who has ADHD, then perhaps they will have a chance. People with ADHD can move just as fast as vampires."

The superior blinked. "Is that so?"

"Yes. We've consulted some experts on the matter."

"You said you didn't contact the Guardians."

"We didn't, but Detectives Zelda and Julian probably have."

"What?" The superior grabbed the podium. "Are you working with them?"

"Yes. We're over our heads. They know what they're doing. They don't have a problem asking for help when they know they're in trouble."

The superior stared at them. The tension grew in the room to the point that reports kept taking pictures and notes on the scene unfolding before everyone.

"How could you contact those detectives?"

"We needed help and they are good detectives."

"Don't you care about your jobs?"

"Yes."

"Then you need to stop talking to those misfits. They don't follow the rules."

The officer sighed. "It's not against the rules to ask for outside help from experts. Detectives Zelda and Julian are experts who know that too. They called for expert help when we had a dangerous werewolf on the loose. If the Guardian hadn't shown up, there would have been more dead than we had. We know we need help dealing with a dangerous vampire. Does it make sense to fire people who are competent? I don't think so. Or perhaps you don't like the detectives because of other more personal reasons."

Gasps were heard throughout the room. Officers tried to hush the one who had spoken.

The superior growled. "How dare you! Zelda is a hard and stuck up woman! Julian is a child who refuses to grow up!"

"Finally, we hear the truth from you. You fired them for those reasons, which is illegal. Not because they broke a rule by asking the Guardians for help. Perhaps you need to be fired from your job."

Many reporters cheered. A few officers started to smile. Others were silent and frowning.

The assistant chief approached the podium. "I'm sorry but this press conference is now over. We thank you all for coming."

"How dare you!" The chief growled at the newcomer.

"Sir, calm down."

"No, you calm down!"

The assistant chief made some hand motions. A few officers came over and arrested the chief.

The assistant chief continued, "I'm sorry, sir, but we can't have this here. If you can't behave and threaten to fire employees because they contacted the Guardians whom you refused to believe in, then we will have to suspend you and investigate your actions."

"This is an outrage!"

The officers took the chief away. The reporters took pictures and more notes. They filed out to avoid any stink eyes from the police force. The officers on the case sighed. They still had their jobs and plenty of work to do.

Once the reports were all gone, someone said, "I hope Detectives Zelda and Julian can solve this case."

"I hope they live through it."

Many cheered on the detectives. Others were silent. They were confused as to what was happening inside the police station. They once believed it was the detectives who were foolish and that's why they were fired. Now many weren't so sure anymore.

Many went back to work saying how much they were hoping Detectives Zelda and Julian would survive and save the people of Tigerwood again.

Chapter 9 The Trap

Cynthia's laugh was haunting and much too loud for Zeta. She felt helpless in the vampire's arms. She felt her braces and the world slowed down around her. She could see Sam and Peter fighting over her. She heard the glass shattered. She saw the vampire fairy and her best friends standing behind her.

Felicia raised her wings and bared her fangs. She hissed at Peter and Cynthia. Sam hissed and bared his fangs at Peter. Zeta blinked. She watched as everything slowed down for her. She carefully undid her braces and pulled them off slowly without alerting Cynthia.

She held her braces in her hands. She raised them and spun around as best and as fast as she could. The vampire had her restrained, but the impact of the braces wasn't pleasant even for someone who didn't fear dying. Cynthia screamed as the braces cut her arms. She let go of the elf.

Felicia flew into the apartment and grabbed Cynthia. Zeta ran out to the balcony to her friends. She collapsed moments later. Julian caught her and gently set her down. He and Zelda put Zeta's braces back on her legs.

Julian smiled at her as he and Zelda got Zeta back on her feet. "Zeta, that was brave. I didn't know you could move like that."

Zeta caught her breath. "I'm not sure what happened. Everything just slowed down and I realized my braces could be weapons if I could get them off."

Zelda smiled. "Good thinking."

The trio looked into the apartment.

"Jul, I wish you brought your hoverboard."

"So, do I, Zel."

Zeta bit her lip. "So, now what do we do? Can we call for backup?"

Julian shrugged his shoulders.

Zelda said, "Who would we call? The Guardians are here. They're fighting the bad vampires right now."

Zeta gasped. "What about the police?"

Julian and Zelda blinked.

"Well, why not? They call you whenever they're unsure of a case. They consult you and ask for your help. Can't we ask them for help? Couldn't they fly overhead and get us out of here?"

Zelda said, "Uh, I'd be afraid to bring anyone else into this fight. Those are vampires who will kill us all if they can."

Julian said, "Yeah, I'm all for keeping the death count down."

Zeta sighed. "Good point."

Cynthia struggled in Felicia's arms. Cynthia was bleeding. She ground her teeth. "Let me go!"

"Nope." Felicia slammed Cynthia into a wall.

Cynthia fell down unconscious. Felicia flew back to Sam and Peter. She grabbed Peter and threw him into the wall near his mother. He hit the wall and fell down to the floor unconscious. Sam and Felicia quickly found some rope and tied up Peter and Cynthia as tightly as they could.

The elves on the balcony applauded. Sam and Felicia turned to glance at them. The Guardians turned back to the dangerous vampires.

Sam asked, "When is daybreak?"

Zelda checked her tablet. She blinked. "In an hour."

Sam said, "Good. We're going to leave these two on the balcony."

Sam and Felicia dragged the two dangerous vampires to the balcony. The elf trio stepped out of the way just inside the apartment.

Zeta asked, "Is this a good thing to do?"

Felicia answered, "They're too dangerous. They can't be reasoned with. It's safer to expose them to the sun than to try to change them."

Zeta nodded.

Julian said, "Zane didn't kill the dangerous werewolf he fought. Instead Zane handcuffed him and took him away with him."

Sam sighed. "Zane knew what he was doing and knew he could subdue the werewolf. When vampires get into blood lust, they are unreasonable. Nothing helps. We've dealt with others in this state and they won't stop fighting until they die."

Zeta said, "Oh! I didn't realize it was that bad."

Sam sighed. "It can be. Becoming a vampire can be traumatic. It was for both of us. But our Guardian training saved us in the end."

Felicia landed next to Sam. She lowered her wings. "I remember my transformation being awful. I'm glad Claire Rose grabbed me after I was bitten and took me to Sam. We were separated because he had been bitten and knew he was going to die. He sacrificed himself to save Claire Rose and Lady Adele."

"Then I became one of them. I thought I was dying at first. I contacted Doctor Butterfly and sent him all the blood samples he wanted. He confirmed what had happened to me. I was too afraid to go near anyone for a long time."

"Except that you hung out in the woods where Claire Rose was exiled. You saved her and me from a tiger."

"You remember that I yelled at both of you to get away from me."

Felicia nodded. "He helped me to get adjusted. Claire Rose helped out too. She was the first one who tossed us bags of donated blood before she would try to talk to us about anything."

"We haven't had to hunt since them."

"We make sure we have access to donated blood or synthetic blood. It keeps the blood lust away."

Zeta nodded. "This is going to be quite a book."

The sun started to rise. Cynthia and Peter opened their eyes.

They struggled in their bonds. They growled at the invaders in their apartment. They tried to get out of the sunlight. They rolled on the broken glasses, which caused both of them to bleed. They screamed.

"Get us out of here!" yelled Cynthia.

"Damn you all!" yelled Peter.

The sun continued to rise. Sam and Felicia stayed inside. She stepped closer to him. They held on to each other. Julian and Zelda both put their arms around Zeta. Cynthia and Peter screamed until their bodies vaporized.

Zeta said, "So, how are you, Felicia and Sam, going to get out of here?"

"We have to wait until the sun goes down."

Zeta blinked. "Can't you just wear hats?"

The vampires looked at the elves.

Felicia asked, "Where would you get an idea like that?"

"Peter wore a hat the first time we met."

Sam and Felicia looked at each other. They looked into each other's eyes. "Let's not…"

The elves smiled.

Sam said, "We all need to write up some sort of reports. We could just get started since we're all here. Then you three can leave when you're ready."

Chapter 10 Reports

At the police station, the officers were shocked to get reports from Detectives Zelda and Julian and from the Guardians. They looked at each other with gaping mouths. They blinked, closed their mouths and smiled.

"Well, Detectives Zelda and Julian have done it again."

"Yes, they saved us all and Zeta will write another book about this one."

"I can't wait for the book. She tends to put in details which are omitted from the reports."

The assistant chief came over. "I have read the reports."

The officers were too afraid to say anything.

"I think it's better to work with Detectives Zelda and Julian. I don't even mind the Guardians. I hate to admit it, but we're not equipped to deal with these kinds of people such as were creatures and vampires."

"So, we can continue to work with Detectives Zelda and Julian?"

"Yes. I'm considering asking them back, but perhaps this is a better arrangement for them."

The officers sighed in relief. "What about the Guardians?"

The assistant chief sighed. "We need to work with them. They are real and have knowledge and personnel that we don't have."

The officers smiled. "I'm sure there's a way of contacting

them and asking for their help. I'm sure they'll send someone to help out the police station."

The assistant chief nodded. "I will go do that. In the meantime, our chief is still suspended. We've been investigating and it's not looking good."

"Will you be promoted?"

"Me? I hadn't thought about it. I don't know how to answer that…"

"One thing at a time. Go contact the Guardians and work with them. It will be a whole new era for this station."

"Yeah. Protect and serve." The assistant chief left.

The officers watched him leave wondering what his next move would be. He got into his office and closed the door. He did a quick little internet search for the Guardians and found a site where he could contact them. He gave his name, job title and requested help from them to help the police with dangerous criminals that were vampires and were creatures.

He sat back and sighed. Things were moving too fast for him to process everything. He wasn't sure he wanted to be the chief of the police. Yet, he didn't think he could say no if he was asked to take over. He blinked and his computer beeped at him.

The Guardians had contacted him and let him know they were sending someone over to help them with those cases. He blinked. "Wow. I'm so glad you're real and not just legend."

Sam and Felicia were sitting at the dinning table with Julian, Zelda and Zeta. All were busy on their reports. They all had just agreed to sent copies to the police. They wrote out the main points and went over those points with each other.

It didn't take them very long. Sam and Felicia sent theirs to the Guardian archives and to the police. Zelda and Julian sent theirs to the police. They also gave Sam and Felicia copies as the vampires gave the detectives their reports.

Felicia was still working on her tablet computer. "Zeta, I'm giving you access to the Guardian archives. Some of the information there is what you're already familiar with. Much of it probably is information you've never seen before."

Zeta smiled. "Thanks. I'm sure it will be helpful."

Felicia smiled back. "I know you need access. Some of these cases could become impossible if you don't have enough information. Oh, and I see the assistant chief of police has decided to contact us for help. Someone has just been assigned to this work."

Zelda said, "So, the police now have a Guardian liaison to help them with the seemingly impossible cases."

Felicia continued. "Yes. And this assistant chief of police has authorized the other officers to work with you too. He might be inclined to hire you back."

Zelda shook her head. "That's okay."

Julian smiled. "I like our agency."

Felicia said, "It's up to you of course."

Zeta said, "I take it, we're done with our reports now?" She covered her mouth as she yawned.

Felicia smiled. "Yeah, we're done. You three should get out of here. Get some sleep."

Zeta asked, "Do vampires need sleep?"

Felicia laughed. "Yes." She glanced at Sam. "Sam and I will bet getting some soon. After you all leave."

The elves put away their tablets and stood up. They all stretched.

Julian looked at his friend. "I hope we can walk home safely."

Zeta giggled. "I'm sure we'll make it." She took his hand.

The elves waved goodbye and left the apartment to a pair of vampires who were smiling at them. Once the elves were gone, the vampires wasted no time. They reached for each other and soon they were stroking and kissing each other.

The three elves took the lift to the street level. Soon they found themselves in bright sunlight. They blinked and waited for their eyes to adjust. They walked down the street together. None of them expected much of anything. They all had bags under their eyes. They were sluggish, but they kept moving. They all wanted to go home and crawl into their beds.

They got to the police station and saw there was a press conference in front of the building. The assistant chief was standing at the podium. The elves stopped to listen.

The assistant chief said, "Welcome, everyone. We the police force are transitioning. Unfortunately, we had to suspend the chief due to some questionable and perhaps illegal activities of his. We are still investigating him. For now, I am acting chief. As my first act, I would like to state that we will continue to work with Detectives Zelda and Julian. My second act is to welcome a Guardian liaison to help us with tough cases which endanger all our lives as this last one did.

"Detectives Zelda and Julian have our gratitude. They solved the case and caught those responsible. They worked with the Guardians because it was two vampires. They risked their lives. I don't know where they are now. I haven't asked them to come back because I thought they liked their own agency better than being on the force. I don't have any problem with their independence."

"They're here! Yeah. Right there!"

Soon everyone was looking at Zelda, Julian and Zeta. They were too tired to respond other than wave as people took their pictures. They tried to smile as they stifled yawns.

The assistant chief smiled at them. "Welcome, Detectives Zelda and Julian and Zeta. We're glad you could make it today. We look forward to working with you in the future."

Julian shouted, "We're here for the people of Tigerwood."

People cheered.

Zelda said, "Let's get out of here." She waved some more.

Julian and Zeta waved. Then the trio turned to leave the area hoping no one would follow. A few reporters tried to chase them and ask questions.

"Please, let the trio leave. They look pretty tired. They've been up all night to save us. Let's let them rest for now. You can interview them later."

The reporters stopped and let the trio go. People still shouted their gratitude. The trio walked away.

It seemed to be an eternity before they found their shared home. Finally they reached the gate and let themselves in. The gate shut behind them.

Zelda reached her tiny house. She opened the door. "Goodnight, you two."

Julian and Zeta said, "Goodnight." They went to Zeta's tiny house.

Julian followed Zeta inside. She walked to her bed and took off her braces. She set them down where they belonged. She crawled under the covers. He followed moments later and crawled under the covers. He wrapped his arms around her waist and they went to sleep with smiles plastered on their faces.

Chapter 11 A New Book

Zelda, Julian and Zeta sat around the fire pit. They had slept for much of the day. Yet, they were still tired. No one wanted to talk just yet. They yawned at different times.

Zeta spoke up, "Have you two noticed how many messages we have been getting lately?"

Zelda and Julian nodded.

"I think we need to hire someone to answer those messages so we can focus on our work."

Julian said, "Good point. You need to write and research. Having to answer all those messages would be bad for us."

Zelda blinked. "I hope that person doesn't need to work here."

Zeta smiled. "They can work from their own home. We just need to set up a general box for most of the messages and a phone line. Things of that sort. That will make it easier for them to answer and take messages and sort out what we don't need to hear versus good jobs to take on."

Zelda said, "I like it. We need to hire someone soon. Our popularity is too good right now."

Julian asked, "But who? How will we know they are the right person for the job?"

Zeta answered, "Someone who doesn't mind answering all the messages. Someone who likes to be around to people or at least talking to them in one way or another all the time."

Julian smiled. "That's not you, Zeta."

"Nope."

Zelda smiled. "Let's place an ad now and see who responds."

They worked on the ad and posted it immediately. They set their tablets down and waited. They didn't want to do anything else for now. Their tablets beeped with messages. They groaned and checked to see what they were.

Zelda said, "Well, that didn't take long for people to respond to our ad."

Julian said, "I think some of these are just fans. I'm not sure they would be candidates."

Zelda nodded. "What about this one? Jaema Sparks. Her resume is impressive."

Julian smiled. "She has the experience and she knows how to work remotely. She's also a big fan of us."

Zeta smiled. "Let's just interview her."

Zelda blinked. "Now?"

Zeta said, "Why not? Let's get this over with. I want to go back to sleep soon without worrying about the messages."

Julian said, "Okay. I'm ready. Zelda?"

"Alright." Zelda contacted Jaema.

Jaema's face appeared on all three screens at once. "Hello, Xenocryst Agency. I'm Jaema. Let's see. I see Zeta the writer, Julian the detective and Zelda the detective. A trio of elves who get along well and save Tigerwood as if it was second nature for them."

Zelda, Julian and Zeta all smiled at her.

"Hello, Jaema. We are happy to see your experience will be helpful with what we need. I'm sure you're not surprised with our popularity now, we are getting too many messages to answer. Some are ones we don't even need to see. What we need is someone to monitor all the communications and let us know about jobs or possible jobs. You don't need to tell us about the rest of the messages."

Jaema nodded. "That's easy enough. Do you have a phone line?"

Julian answered, "Not for just the agency. We know we need that now."

Jaema nodded. "I can set up a dedicated phone line for the agency. I will answer it during specific hours and have a professional message for when the line is not monitored. I can check those messages along with monitoring the messages from the site. I think it might be easier if I have access to your appointment book too. That way I can set up meetings with clients."

Julian looked at his partners. "That would be helpful. We hadn't thought of that one."

Jaema smiled. "I know a good one to use that we can access. I'll set up the account for it." She paused to look at all three. She relaxed knowing they were elves as she was. "I can start tomorrow if that works for you."

Julian blinked. Zelda blinked. Zeta blinked. They all looked at each other. Then back to Jaema on their screens.

Zelda said, "I think that would great. We need your expertise now." She yawned. "Excuse me. We didn't get to sleep last night and we've slept most of the day today."

Jaema nodded. "Perfectly alright. I know you had to deal with vampires last night."

Zelda continued. "We will send you our contact info and let you set up the accounts for a phone line and the scheduling book. We may or may not keep regular office hours, but you can as much as possible so people have a way of contacting us. We don't expect you to work all the time."

Jaema smiled. "I look forward to working with you three. Zeta, when is the next book coming out?"

Zeta smiled. "I need to draft it. I have notes on it and the reports. So, that's what I'll be doing tomorrow. It will take some time before the book is released."

Jaema nodded. "I look forward to reading it. I've read the others and enjoyed your adventures."

Julian smiled. "We know you're a fan."

Jaema laughed. "I am, but I will still be professional. I'm looking forward to getting to know the three of you better. I do hope I can make your work easier."

They discounted and yawned.

Julian said, "Well, I do hope she works out."

Zelda said, "I hope so too. She seems pleasant enough."

Zeta said, "I hope she doesn't become a liability. She is beautiful as I'm sure you both noticed."

Julian chuckled.

Zelda yawned and smiled. "Yes, she is. I hope she knows how to defend herself."

Julian said, "If she doesn't, then we can pay for her to learn."

Zelda said, "Zeta could use some of that training too."

Zeta said, "Of course I need that. I can take the classes with Jaema."

They stood up. Zelda went to her house.

Julian looked at Zeta. "Zeta, perhaps I should put the tent away. Would you mind sharing your house with me all the time?"

Zeta blinked. "No, I don't mind. Just don't leave it messy. I don't know if there's room for everything."

"We can work on that tomorrow. I'm too tired to do anything else tonight other than crawl into bed and cuddle up to you."

"Okay." She walked inside her house.

"Wait, you didn't put on your braces, did you?"

She shook her head no.

"You seem to be doing okay."

"Well, I'm slower without the braces, and I still need the railing. But I think I'm doing better now."

He smiled at her.

The trio slept the night away knowing they had solved another case and saved many people who lived in the City of Tigerwood. They didn't think about doing any other kind of work. They dreamed away and rested up after the recent events.

They were sleeping soundly knowing not all vampires were dangerous. It was as comforting as knowing not all were creatures were dangerous either. Many could learn to live among others without causing them any harm. And it was comforting to know they didn't have to worry about all the messages that piled up for them any time of day now.